Copyright © Karen Chaplin (2(

A CIP catalogue record for this title is available from the British Library.

ISBN 9798837151057 (Paper back)

Kindle ebook also available

Email: iamdog2020@hotmail.com
Facebook: www.facebook.com/ iamdog2020/
Instagram: www.instagram.com/iam.dog2020/?hl=en

First Published (2022)

Stay safe online. Any website addresses listed in this book are correct at the time of going to print. Please be aware that online content can be subject to change and websites can contain content not suitable for children. It is advised that all children are supervised when using the internet.

Karen lives with her family in the beautiful Forest of Dean. She is originally from Bristol but moved over the bridge for a more rural setting. She enjoys walks in the woods with her family and dog and loves nothing better than being surrounded by nature.

Karen has spent many years working in Primary schools, but has had many interesting jobs in her time. Once she had a job making body parts! Now she works in the engineering industry.

Karen's children are now older, so has freed up a bit of time so she can start fulfilling a childhood dream of writing children's books.

"I am Dog" was published in 2020 and after its success Karen has decided to create another choose your own adventure story. These stories are designed to encourage decision making in young readers and to help give them confidence with numeracy. The rhyming text is designed to help with reading and it's fun to read. The illustrations are busy and bright to engage young minds and get them asking questions and get their imaginations bubbling. Karen says that she wishes books like this were available when her children were younger. As decision making at a young age is so important.

Hello, little Mouse,
With your eyes so bright
With your fur so soft
And your feet so light.

Do you want some fun?
Is that why you're here?
Take a look in these pages,
Go on...have a peer.

Please go to page 2

1

Today, little Mouse
You can choose what to do.
You can go to the beach
You can go to the zoo.

Hedgehog says,

"Under the gardens great fun!"

But Bat insists,

"The abandoned house must be done!"

Maybe today you
Are tired like Snail?
Or bursting with joy
Like Dog chasing his tail?

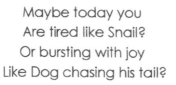

So gather your friends
And choose what to do.
There are lots of adventures,
Waiting for you.

What do you choose, Mouse?
Got to the beach-page 3
Go to the zoo-page 4
Go and explore the garden-page 5
Visit the abandoned house-page 6
Or go home for a nap-page 34

2

Your little pink feet
Feel the heat of the sand
So you run to the water,
Then back on the land.

Can you see the Pier?
Bridging out to the sea.
The gulls shout out loud
Eating food that is free.

What do you want to do, Mouse?
Try your luck at the sand castle competition-page 7
Go to the pier-page 8
Have you got a hungry tummy?-page 10
Go scuba diving and see some fish-page 16

Or leave the beach and...
Go to the zoo-page 4
See what's in the garden-page 5
Go to the abandoned house-page 6
Go home for a nap-page 34

3

You arrive at the zoo,
Feeling very excited.
Every one of your friends
Is equally delighted!

Dog lifts you up,
For a much better view.
Now you can see
All the things you may do.

KEEP OFF
THE GRASS

PLEASE

PARK
INSECTS
CAFE

Who shall you visit first, Mouse?
Visit your old friend Elephant-page 12
Visit Insect World-page 13
Visit sleepy Sloth-page 14
Go and have your photo taken-page 15

Or leave the zoo and...
Go to the beach-page 3
Go to the garden at home-page 5
Go to the abandoned house-page 6
Go home for a nap-page 34

4

You all love the garden,
Great places to hide.
You can scurry around,
And then scamper inside.

There's an old oak tree,
You can look and explore.
Or under the garden,
Discovering more.

Where are you going to explore first, Mouse?
Go under the garden and explore the tunnels-page 21
Go inside the old oak tree-page 23

Or leave the garden and...
Visit the beach-page 3
Visit the zoo-page 4
Go to the abandoned house-page 6
Go home for a nap-page 34

5

You get your bucket.
You get your spade.
You dig a hole.
That's how they're made.

You build up walls.
Then dig a moat,
The turrets stand grand
And you float a small boat.

The sun's shining down,
But your castle is done.
You place shells and flags,
Then get out of the sun.

Did you use a dry mix to build your sandcastle? – page 9
Or did you use a wet mix to build it? – page 11

7

Because you're so tiny,
You tread carefully.
Skipping over the gaps,
That look down to the sea.

There's a small, bright red train
That goes chuffing along.
Lots of lights, lots of noise,
A familiar song.

You go to the rail.
Feel the wind on your face.
Your smile is so big.
What a brilliant place!

You see the arcade,
A small roller coaster.
More smells, more sounds,
You decide to move closer.

What next, Mouse?

Go on the roller coaster-page 19
Go on the claw/grab machine-page 20

8

Such an amazing creation,
That stands tall and proud.
You love all the cheering
And the noise from the crowd.

First prize *and* a trophy!
"Well done!" they all say.
Now what shall you do?
For the rest of the day.

What next, Mouse?

Go to the pier-page 8
Go and have some food-page 10
Have a go at scuba diving-page 16

Or leave the beach and...
Go to the zoo-page 4
Go home to the garden-page 5
Visit the abandoned house-page 6
Go home for a nap-page 34

9

What food do you fancy?
How hungry are you?
Chips, ice cream, some candy?
A chocolate bar too?

You fill up your belly.
You're ready to go.
But your friends are still eating,
They're terribly slow!

What next, Mouse?
Have a go at the sandcastle competition-page 7
Go to the pier-page 8
Go scuba diving-page 16

Or leave the beach and...
Go to the zoo-page 4
Go home to the garden-page 5
Visit the abandoned house-page 6
Go home for a nap-page 34

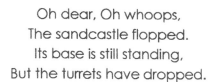

Oh dear, Oh whoops,
The sandcastle flopped.
Its base is still standing,
But the turrets have dropped.

The sides slide down
And into the moat.
One of the flags,
Has splatted your boat.

Never mind, Mouse.
You can't win them all.
It's a little bit sad,
That it no longer stands tall.

What do you want to do next, Mouse?
Visit the pier-page 8
Go and have some food-page 10
Go scuba diving-page 16

Or leave the beach and...
Go to the zoo-page 4
Go home to the garden-page 5
Visit the abandoned house-page 6
Go home for a nap-page 34

11

Elephant waves
As he sees you come near.
Trumpeting his trunk,
And flapping his ears.

He's such a good friend
You chat and you play.
You all laugh so much,
What a treat to the day!

What do you want to do after you say goodbye to Elephant?
Visit Insect World-page 13
Visit sleepy Sloth-page 14
Go and have your photo taken-page 15

Or leave the zoo and...
Go to the beach-page 3
Go home to the garden-page 5
Go and visit the abandoned house-page 6
Go home for a nap-page 34

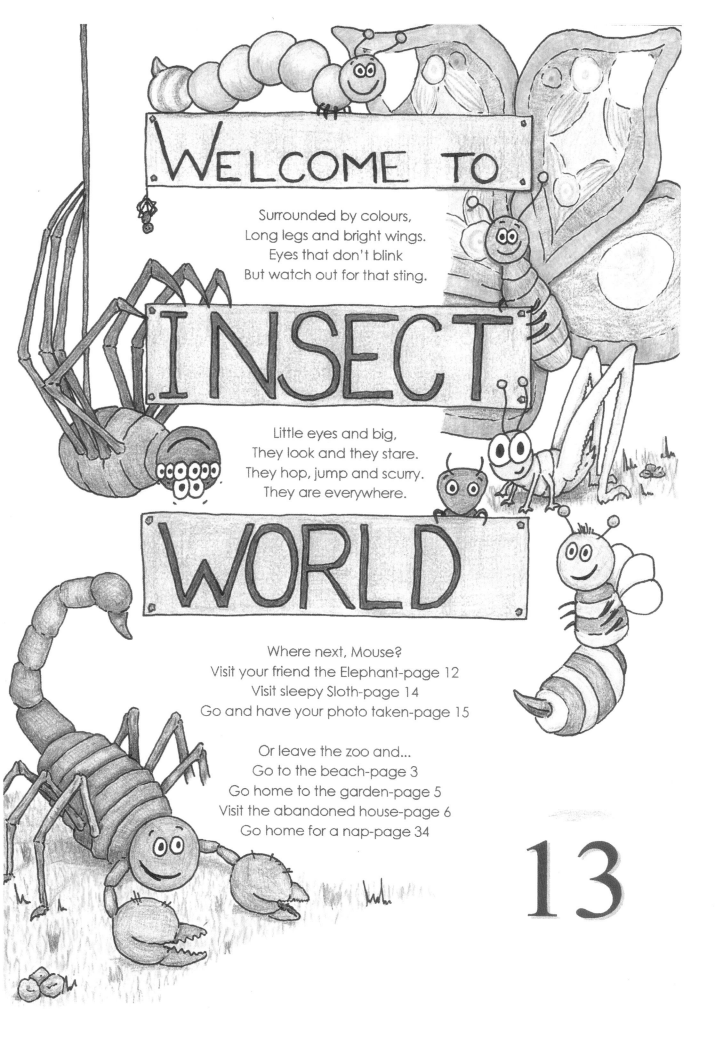

WELCOME TO

Surrounded by colours,
Long legs and bright wings.
Eyes that don't blink
But watch out for that sting.

INSECT

Little eyes and big,
They look and they stare.
They hop, jump and scurry.
They are everywhere.

WORLD

Where next, Mouse?
Visit your friend the Elephant-page 12
Visit sleepy Sloth-page 14
Go and have your photo taken-page 15

Or leave the zoo and...
Go to the beach-page 3
Go home to the garden-page 5
Visit the abandoned house-page 6
Go home for a nap-page 34

13

"Hey Sloth, you awake?"
You keep your voice low.
Is she asleep?
Or is she *that* slow?

Snail gives her a nudge.
Duck gives her a peck.
Sloth yawns and then stretches,
And scratches her neck.

Her eyes remain closed.
So you scurry away.
You'll see your friend Sloth
On a 'not so lazy' day.

What next, Mouse?
Visit your dear friend Elephant-page 12
Visit Insect World-page 13
Go and have your photo taken-page 15

Or leave the zoo and...
Go to the beach-page 3
Go home to the garden-page 5
Visit the abandoned house-page 6
Go home for a nap-page 34

14

A giggle and a nudge,
Shuffling for space,
Getting in position,
Pull a funny face.

What next, Mouse?
Visit your friend the Elephant-page 12
Visit Insect World-page 13
Visit sleepy Sloth-page 14

Or leave the zoo and...
Go to the beach-page 3
Go home to the garden-page 5
Visit the abandoned house-page 6
Go home for a nap-page 34

15

You put on your flippers,
And all of your gear.
Mind your long tail,
And don't crush your ear!

Once in the water,
Diving down deep.
It's like another world,
With cool creatures to meet.

But there's so much more to do, Mouse. What next?
Try your luck at the sandcastle competition-page 7
Visit the pier-page 8
Go and have some yummy food-page 10

Or leave the beach and...
Go to the zoo-page 4
Go home to the garden-page 5
Visit the abandoned house-page 6
Go home for a nap-page 34

16

You go up to Mole,
And ask for advice,
Mole is so kind,
Mole is so nice.

It doesn't matter,
That he cannot see.
He's an amazing guide
And he guides you all free.

You thank kind Mole,
And go on your way.
Back to the garden,
Mole saved the day!!!

Do you want to explore the old oak tree?-page 23

Or leave the garden and...
Go to the beach-page 3
Go to the zoo-page 4
Visit the abandoned house-page 6
Go home for a nap-page 34

17

You decide to go up
To the loft at the top.
Creaky stairs, blackened walls,
But you're not going to stop.

Bat flutters ahead,
And you scurry behind.
As you enter the loft,
Who knows what you'll find.

What's that in the corner?
That oddly white shape?
What's that sound? Can you hear!
That it's starting to make!

Your eyes are so wide,
And your heart beats so fast,
You run down so quickly,
And you're outside at last.

You decide to leave the abandoned house.
Where to next, Mouse?

Go to the beach-page 3
Go to the zoo-page 4
Go home to the garden-page 5
Go home for a nap-page 34

18

This ride is so fast,
Hold on. Off you go!
Zooming round corners,
It doesn't go slow.

It climbs to the roof,
And out through a door,
Over the sea,
Then back in once more.

What next, Mouse?
Try your luck at the claw/grab machine-page 20

Or back to the beach to...
Have a go at the sand castle competition-page 7
Go and have some food-page 10
Scuba diving sounds fun-page 16

Or leave the beach and...
Go to the zoo-page 4
Go home to the garden-page 5
Visit the abandoned house-page 6
Go home for a nap-page 34

You press the UP arrow,
The grabby hand moves.
You're eyes are so big,
Which cute toy shall you choose?

You move the claw slowly,
Slightly off to the right.
It stops. Shoots down.
In the toys, out of sight.

You're holding your breath.
And daren't move your eyes.
As the claw comes back up.
Is it holding a prize?

Out of the bundle,
Pops a cute teddy bear.
Well done, little Mouse.
He's like you, with grey hair!

Do you want to go on the roller coaster-page 19

Or go back to the beach and...
Enter the sandcastle competition-page 7
Go and have some yummy food-page 10
Give scuba diving a go-page 16

Or leave the beach and...
Go to the zoo-page 4
Go home to the garden-page 5
Visit the abandoned house-page 6
Go home for a nap-page 34

20

There are so many tunnels,
Hidden below,
Which way to turn?
Which way to go?

The roots from above,
Tickle your nose.
And something below,
Tickle your toes.

Your eyes have adjusted,
To the darkness around.
The noises are quiet,
Just a muffling sound.

The bugs that you pass,
They go to and fro.
You stop at a junction,
Which way to go?

Turn left-page 22

Turn right-page 24

Or go straight ahead-page 26

21

You decide to go left,
The tunnel gets wide.
There's a hole in the wall,
But there's nothing inside.

The floor feels damp,
And soggy to touch,
You're a tough little Mouse,
It doesn't bother you much.

Up ahead you can see,
Some light shining through,
Yeah – back to the garden,
Now, what shall you do?

Explore the old oak tree?-page 23

Or leave the garden and...
Go to the beach-page 3
Go to the zoo-page 4
Visit the abandoned house-page 6
Go home for a nap-page 34

22

This tree is so old,
It's rotten inside.
But strangely one half,
Is still strong and alive.

Your whiskers get tickled,
Your nose starts to itch.
Must be all these webs,
And these dangly bits.

You climb for a bit,
Then look out a knot,
It makes a cool window,
You can see quite a lot.

You continue to climb,
Right to the top.
Wow – What a view!
It's a beautiful spot.

Do you want to jump from the top of the tree?-page 25
Or would you rather climb down?-page 27

23

You turn to the right,
The tunnel gets thinner.
Good job you're so tiny,
And had a small dinner.

You run on ahead,
In a bit of a rush,
You're looking for light,
In the darkness and dust.

You suddenly stop,
And wait for your friends.
You're hoping the exit,
Is just round the bend.

Please go to page 28

24

You're a daredevil Mouse!
But you can't just jump,
It's a long way down,
You'll land with a thump.

You decide it is safer,
To glide – not just fall.
So you grab a large leaf,
And hold tight with your paw.

You run and you leap,
It's like you can fly.
Your little feet flap,
You're so high in the sky.

You glide back and forth,
And slowly come down.
It's nice when you land,
Safe and sound, on the ground.

Explore the underground tunnels-page 21

Or leave the garden and...
Go to the beach-page 3
Go to the zoo-page 4
Visit the abandoned house-page 6
Go home for a nap-page 34

25

You decide to head straight,
And your friends - they agree.
But watch out for that root,
That's attached to a tree!

You tumble and fall,
But you're tough – you're okay.
You brush yourself off,
And you hurry away.

The tunnel bends left,
And then a bit right,
You go round the corner,
And then out of sight.

Please go to page 28

26

You start your climb down,
Go careful – don't slip.
Grabbing so tight,
Use your tail on that bit.

You're clever at this,
Like a little trapeze.
Balancing careful,
With the slightest of ease.

Almost there, Mouse.
A small jump and you're down.
Your friends give a cheer,
When you're safe on the ground.

Do you want to explore the tunnels under the garden-page 21

Or leave the garden and...
Go to the beach-page 3
Go to the zoo-page 4
Visit the abandoned house-page 6
Go home for a nap-page 34

27

Ask a colony of ants for directions?-page 30
Ask Mole for directions?-page 17

The sun goes away as
You walk up the path.
Empty pots, long grass,
And a broken birdbath.

You squeeze through the door,
And tip-toe inside,
It's dirty and dark,
Smells like something has died.

Are you brave enough to...
Go up into the loft-page 18
Go upstairs-page 31
Go into the cellar-page 32
Go along to the kitchen-page 33

Or is it too scary and you want to leave and...
Go to the beach-page 3
Go to the zoo-page 4
Go home to the garden-page 5
Go home and take a nap-page 34

29

You decide to ask Mole for directions-page 17

30

The curtains are shut,
And every door,
The wallpapers peeling,
There's a hole in the floor.

The wind, as it whistles,
Through an old cracked window,
Or is something howling?
From somewhere below.

Where next, Mouse?
Up to the loft-page 18
Down to the cellar-page 32
Down to the kitchen-page 33

Or leave the house and...
Go to the beach-page 3
Go to the zoo-page 4
Go home to the garden-page 5
Go home to sleep-page 34

31

Cobwebs that tickle,
And dust makes you sneeze.
You're covered in dirt,
A cool breeze makes you freeze!

Toys in the corner,
An old picture frame,
A mirror, a chair,
A piano, a game.

A little bit spooky,
Let's get out of here,
It gives you the creeps,
And fills you with fear.

Where next, Mouse?
Up, all the way to the loft-page 18
Upstairs-page 31
Into the kitchen-page 33

Or leave the house and...
Go to the beach-page 3
Go to the zoo-page 4
Go home to the garden-page 5
Go home for a nap-page 34

32

What's that you hear?
As you go in the kitchen.
You listen and learn,
It's just the tap dripping.

The floor is all sticky,
There are pots, there are pans,
There's a rat in the cupboard,
He waves out his hand.

You wave back at Rat and...
Go to the loft-page 18
Go upstairs-page 31
Go down to the cellar-page 32

Or leave the house and...
Go to the beach-page 3
Go to the zoo-page 4
Go home to the garden-page 5
Go home for a nap-page 34

33

Printed in Great Britain
by Amazon

82416737R00022